GIRLS
Pool

Holly Smith Dinbergs

illustrated by
Monika Maddock

RISING ★ STARS

First published in Great Britain by
RISING STARS UK LTD 2005
76 Farnaby Road, Bromley, BR1 4BH

Reprinted 2006 (twice)

For information visit our website at:
www.risingstars-uk.com

British Library Cataloguing in Publication Data

A CIP record for this book is available from the British Library.

ISBN: 1-905056-17-6

First published in 2005 by
MACMILLAN EDUCATION AUSTRALIA PTY LTD
627 Chapel Street, South Yarra, Australia 3141

Visit our website at www.macmillan.com.au

Associated companies and representatives throughout the world.

Copyright © Holly Smith Dinbergs 2005

Series created by Felice Arena and Phil Kettle
Project Management by Limelight Press Pty Ltd
Cover and text design by Lore Foye
Illustrations by Monika Maddock

Printed and bound in Great Britain by
Mackays of Chatham plc, Chatham, Kent

GIRLS ROCK!
Contents

Jules   Rosa

CHAPTER 1

Early Morning Meet

Jules is upstairs in her bedroom
when her best friend Rosa arrives.
A few seconds later, Rosa throws her
backpack on the bed and flops down
beside the bag.

Jules "You didn't take long to settle
in. Are you comfortable there?"

Rosa laughs, then settles back
onto the pillow on the bed.

Rosa "Are you ready for the school
swimming gala?"
Jules "I think so. I can't believe it's
come around again so quickly."
Rosa "Me neither—I'll be happy
when it's all over."

Jules "I wish you could have slept over here last night."

Rosa "I know, but Dad was afraid we'd talk all night. He said I needed to get a good night's sleep before the gala."

Jules "Remember the last time you stayed over? We didn't go to sleep until almost four in the morning. Mum wasn't happy."

Rosa "It was because of that shadow we saw outside the window."

Jules "The one that turned out to be a harmless cat?"

Rosa "Yes, that fooled us! Let's ask if I can sleep over this weekend."

4

Jules "OK, and we can plan a
midnight raid on the kitchen."

Rosa "Great. I'm putting chocolate
chip cookies at the top of the
search list!"

Jules's mother calls upstairs that
it's time to leave.

Jules "Well, this is it."

Rosa "I'm totally nervous, aren't you? But you don't need to be— you're such a good swimmer. You won nearly every race last year."

Jules "I know, but I had my lucky ankle chain then."

Rosa "How could I forget! You never stop talking about it."

Jules "Well, it was special and I can't believe I lost it."

Rosa "I know, but that won't stop you swimming well. Just remember what Mr. Zammit says."

Jules "As if I ever could. He really drums that chant into us like a Maori war cry or something."

Jules and Rosa "You can do it, I can do it, we all can do it!"

The girls chant all way down the stairs. They race outside to the car where Jules's mother is waiting.

Rosa "Oh, wait! I've left my bag in your room."

Rosa runs back inside. After a few minutes, she still hasn't returned.

Jules (calling out) "Rosa, where are you? We do want to make the first race, don't we?"

A moment later Rosa's back in the car and they all head off to the leisure centre.

CHAPTER 2

Butterfly Babes

Jules says goodbye to her mum.
Then the girls head inside with all
the other competitors.

Jules "Race you to the changing rooms!"

Rosa "You know we're not supposed to run."

Jules "Then let's power walk. The teachers can't get us for that. It's good exercise."

As the girls move off, Jules puts her towel around her shoulders like a cape. Rosa is right behind her.

Rosa "Jules, you look like a
    butterfly—with really long legs."
Jules "What do you mean?"
Rosa "When you walk fast like that,
    the air puffs your towel out like
    butterfly wings."

Jules "Oh, cool, I love butterflies."

Rosa decides to do the same with her towel.

Rosa "Look at us. We're butterfly babes."
Jules "Or pool pals!"

Once in the changing rooms, the girls get into their swimming costumes, then walk out to the pool.

Rosa "Wow! Look how crowded this place is."

Jules "The teachers will call us over soon to start racing. Do you want to get wet first?"

Rosa "OK, let's go together. One, two, three …"

CHAPTER 3

Go Rosa!

After warming up in the water, all the swimmers hop out of the pool, ready to begin the gala.

Rosa "It's almost time for my race."

Jules "You're going to be great."

Rosa "Hope so, but I'm really nervous."

Rosa lines up for her event—the 100-metre freestyle.

Jules "Good luck, Rosa!"

Rosa "I just don't want to come last."

Jules "You won't. Hey look, there's your dad."

Rosa looks up to see her dad and mum in the crowd. They smile and wave at the girls. Rosa walks towards the starting blocks.

Rosa (talking to herself) "I can do it. I can do it."

Rosa and the other swimmers line up at the end of the pool. The starter raises his pistol then *bang!* and Rosa dives in.

Jules "Go, Rosa, go! Go, Rosa, go!"

As Rosa approaches the end of the first lap, Jules screams even louder.

Jules "Rosa, get ready to turn, now turn. One lap to go!"

Rosa touches the wall and turns. She's just behind the fastest swimmer. With less than a metre to go, she reaches for the finishing wall. Jules runs up to her.

Jules "That was amazing!"

Rosa "But I didn't win."

Jules "Yes, but you came second. That's totally cool. I hope I can do that well, even without my lucky ankle chain."

Rosa "You will. You've got to forget about that ankle chain and just go for it."

CHAPTER 4

Jules's Big Moment

An announcement echoes around the pool that the next event is about to begin.

Rosa "Now, it's your race, Jules. Good luck!"

Jules moves to the edge of the pool in lane three. She notices Rosa smiling with her towel around her shoulders like butterfly wings. *Bang!* and Jules dives in.

Rosa (cheering) "Go, Jules, go!"

Jules speeds up the pool and takes the lead. There's a girl in a green swimming costume in the next lane. By the second lap, the girl has moved slightly ahead of her. Jules tries to swim faster.

Rosa "Come on Jules, you're almost winning. I can do it! You can do it! We all ..."

With every stroke, Jules gains on
the girl in the green swimming
costume.

Jules (thinking as she swims along)
"She looks like a crocodile. I can
beat any old crocodile!"

Jules is spurred on even more.
A few seconds later she touches the
wall of the pool with her hand.
She looks up to see Rosa.

Rosa "You won! You won!"

Jules gets out of the pool and the girls jump up and down excitedly, hugging each other.

Jules "This is so cool. I thought that crocodile was going to beat me."

Rosa "Crocodile?"

Jules "Forget it, my eyes were playing tricks on me out there. I can't believe I won that race."

CHAPTER 5

Surprise! Surprise!

After the gala, the girls go back
to Jules's house. They are tired, but
are both really happy about Jules's
win. They race straight upstairs to
Jules's bedroom.

Jules "What's this sign on my door? 'Congratulations'—who did this? And a present. This is so weird. My birthday's not till next week."

Rosa starts to laugh.

Rosa "I did it. I only pretended to leave my bag in your room this morning so I had an excuse to come back and hang up the sign. I made it for you last night because ... well, I just knew that you'd win today."

Jules "But I really thought I'd lose without my lucky ankle chain."

Rosa "Well, there you go, you didn't, you won all by yourself."

Jules smiles and rips the ribbon and wrapping paper off the present.

Jules "Oh, great! Another ankle chain. It's so cool, better than the one I lost. I just love it ... thanks Rosa."

Rosa "It's an early birthday present, a new lucky ankle chain. But I don't think you need it anymore. You rocked today!"

Jules "So did you. This ankle chain is so beautiful. I wish I had something for you."

Rosa "Um ... well, maybe you have."

Jules "Really? What?"

Rosa "How about some chocolate chip cookies?"

Jules

Swimming Lingo

Rosa

butterfly A swimming stroke that requires strong shoulders and stomach muscles.

lane The area of the pool marked off by special ropes where you swim if you compete in a race.

lane lines The dividers used to mark the lanes for a swimming race. They are often special ropes designed to keep the water calm during a race.

lap One length of a pool.

tumble turn When you turn around at the end of the pool after a lap by doing a forward somersault through the water so you end up facing the opposite end of the pool.

GIRLS ROCK!
Swimming Must-dos

☆ Wear a swimming costume when you swim in public.

☆ Don't forget to bring a towel.

☆ Ask your parents for a pair of goggles if you don't like water in your eyes.

☆ Don't breathe underwater. Get a pair of nose plugs if you don't like water in your nose.

☆ If you get a lot of ear infections, wear earplugs in the water.

☆ If you don't want to get your hair wet, wear a cool bathing cap.

☆ Learn to do a tumble turn, especially if you want to set a world record. It's much faster and you look really cool!

☆ Always swim with a friend. It's more fun and if one of you has a problem, the other one can get help.

Swimming Instant Info

 An Olympic sized pool is 50 metres long and 25 metres wide.

 Swimming became an Olympic event in 1908, but women weren't allowed to compete until 1912.

Today, there are 16 swimming races in the Olympic Games.

Anita Lonsborough, Sharon Davies and Sarah Hardcastle have all won Olympic swimming medals for Great Britain.

Elephants can swim up to 32 kilometres a day. They use their trunks as natural snorkels.

Hungarian, Kirsztina Egerszegi, holds the world record for winning the most gold medals in women's swimming at the Olympics. She has won gold medals for the 100 metre backstroke (1992), the 200 metre backstroke (1988, 1992, 1996) and the 400 metre medley (1992).

There are four main swimming strokes: backstroke, breaststroke, butterfly and freestyle.

Kangaroos are excellent swimmers.

The temperature in the pool at the Olympics has to be between 25°C and 28°C.

GIRLS ROCK!
Think Tank

1 If a black-footed penguin, a bottle-nosed dolphin and a tuna fish swam in a race, who would win?

2 Can a butterfly actually swim?

3 How long is an Olympic-sized pool?

4 What's the best kind of towel to use?

5 When should you not take a big breath?

6 How wide is an Olympic-sized pool?

7 Where do swimmers hang out?

8 Where do you wear swimming goggles?

Answers

8 You wear swimming goggles in the pool (or in the ocean).

7 Swimmers hang out by the pool, of course!

6 An Olympic-sized pool is 25 metres wide.

5 You should not take a big breath when you are swimming underwater—unless you are wearing a snorkel or scuba gear.

4 The best kind of towel to use is a dry one!

3 An Olympic-sized pool is 50 metres long.

2 No—a butterfly cannot actually swim.

1 If a black-footed penguin, a bottle-nosed dolphin and a tuna swam in a race together, the penguin would win because it can swim about 40 miles (64 kilometres) per hour. The dolphin would come second and the tuna fish would come last.

How did you score?

- If you got all 8 answers correct, then you're ready to start training for the Olympics. So get your goggles on!

- If you got 6 answers correct, then maybe you can be a lifeguard at the pool (get your safety certificate first!).

- If you got fewer than 4 answers correct, you might want to take a few more swimming lessons or watch from the side of the pool.

Hey Girls!

I love to read and hope you do, too. The first book I really loved was called "Mary Poppins." It was full of magic (well before Harry Potter) and it got me hooked on reading. I went to the library every Saturday and left with a pile of books so heavy I could hardly carry them!

Here are some ideas about how you can make "Pool Pals" even more fun. At school, you and your friends can be actors and put on this story as a play. To bring the story to life, bring in some props from home such as a big towel and an ankle chain. Maybe you can set up an area in the room to look like starting blocks for a pool race.

Who will be Jules? Who will be Rosa? Who will be the narrator? (That's the person who reads the parts between when Jules or Rosa say something.) Once you know who's going to do what, you're ready to act out the story in front of the class. I bet everyone will clap when you are finished. Hey, a talent scout from a television station may be watching!

See if somebody at home will read this story out loud with you. Reading at home is important and a lot of fun as well.

Do you know what my dad used to tell me? "Readers are leaders".

And, remember, Girls Rock!

GIRLS ROCK!
When We Were Kids

Holly *Julie*

Holly talked with Julie,
another *Girls Rock!* author.

Holly "Were you a good swimmer?"

Julie "Yes, I loved it! I was really good at butterfly."

Holly "I used to go to the pool with my friends and look at the cute lifeguards."

Julie "Were you a good swimmer?"

Holly "Well, I was a better diver. I could do a back flip. Did you know that if you don't quite finish a back flip, it's a belly flop?"

Julie "Ouch. I'll stick to butterfly."

Holly "Yes, a butterfly would beat a belly flop any day!"

GIRLS ROCK!
What a Laugh!

Q Why did the swimming star throw her toast out of the window?

A She wanted to see butter fly.

GIRLS ROCK!

Read about the fun
that girls have in these
GIRLS ROCK! titles:

The Sleepover

Pool Pals

Bowling Buddies

Girl Pirates

Netball Showdown

School Play Stars

Diary Disaster

Horsing Around

GIRLS ROCK! books are available from
most booksellers. For mail order information
please call Rising Stars on 01933 443862 or visit
www.risingstars-uk.com